BOBBY AND BEN'S BIRTHDAY PARTY

SOPHIA EDWARDS

Illustrated by Sierra Mon Ann Vidal

To order additional copies of this book, contact:
Xlibris
844-714-8691
www.Xlibris.com
Orders@Xlibris.com

ISBN: Softcover   978-1-6641-6399-7
        EBook   978-1-6641-6398-0

Print information available on the last page

Rev. date: 03/26/2021

BOBBY AND BEN'S BIRTHDAY PARTY

By

SOPHIA EDWARDS

Once upon a time, there lived a boy called Bobby. Bobby was living in a town called Hat Rubbery about fifteen kilometers away from Plymouth.

When Bobby turned five, one day, his mother went to town and bought him a cat. Bobby named the cat Ben and gave his love to it.

The following day, Bobby called his mother, "Mummy, Mummy! When you are going to town tomorrow for shopping, I will go with you."

His mother asked, "What are you going to do there?"

Then Bobby replied, "I am going to buy plates, glasses, and a small mattress for Ben because it did not sleep well yesterday."

His mother was surprised and then said to Bobby, "Hold on for some time. I will buy them for you when I get money."

Bobby replied, "Mummy, I have money. I have ten dollars. Have you forgotten that uncle gave me money when he came from Dorset?"

His mother said, "Oh yes, I now remember! We shall go tomorrow."

The following day, Bobby woke up as early as four o'clock and woke his mother up. His mother said, "Ah, Bobby! It's too early for us to go to shop. Sleep. I will wake you up at six o'clock."

Bobby did not sleep again as he was lying on the bed. When it was six o'clock, his mother woke him from the bed. He took his bath, dressed up, then ran to his mother and said, "Mummy, Mummy, I'm ready."

His mother said, "I'm also ready, and so let's go."

After picking the plates, glasses, and mattress for Ben at a shop, Bobby called for his mother, "Mummy, I have not bought a toothbrush for Ben. It needs brush too."

His mother laughed and said, "Ben will not clean its teeth. It's not a human being."

Bobby said, "Buy toffees for Ben so that when it cries, then I give it to eat."

His mother said," No, Ben cannot eat toffees. It can only eat food."

Bobby then said, "Mummy, go and pay and let's go home. Ben will cry and look for me." His mother went to pay for the items bought, and they went home.

When they reached home, Ben ran to Bobby and started crying, "Meow, meow, meow."

Bobby said, "I told you, Mummy. Look, it's crying." Then he also started crying and picked Ben up.

His mother said, "Don't cry, Ben. Don't cry, Bobby. Don't cry, Bobby. I will give Ben some food so that it does not cry." His mother went to the kitchen and brought rice and stew for Ben. After Ben had finished eating, his mother gave Bobby some food to eat.

Bobby said, "Mummy, it had stopped crying." Bobby went to lay their bed, and they went to bed together.

On every day, after Bobby had finished bathing, he picked Ben up and then combed its hair. They played together in the house, ate, and then went to bed at the same time.

On Bobby's sixth birthday, Mummy called Bobby in the morning and said, "Bobby, today is your sixth birthday. I will organize a party for Ben and you in the evening."

Bobby became very happy, then said to his mother, "Mummy, I am happy to celebrate my birthday party with Ben this time."

Mummy then said, "Get your suit for the party and keep the small suit for Ben." Ha ha ha! And then she said, "Ben will put on a suit today. Oh! Oh! Know it will be nice."

Ten friends of Bobby were invited to that party. Prayer was first said, and after then, drinks were served. Bobby was then called to cut the cake. Bobby said, "Mummy, look at Ben. It's going out as I was called to cut the cake." Mummy went out and brought Ben to the high table. Bobby picked up Ben, and they cut the cake.

His friend shouted, "Happy birthday to Bobby and Ben."

His friend shouted, "Happy birthday to Bobby and Ben."

"Meow, meow, meow," cried Ben.

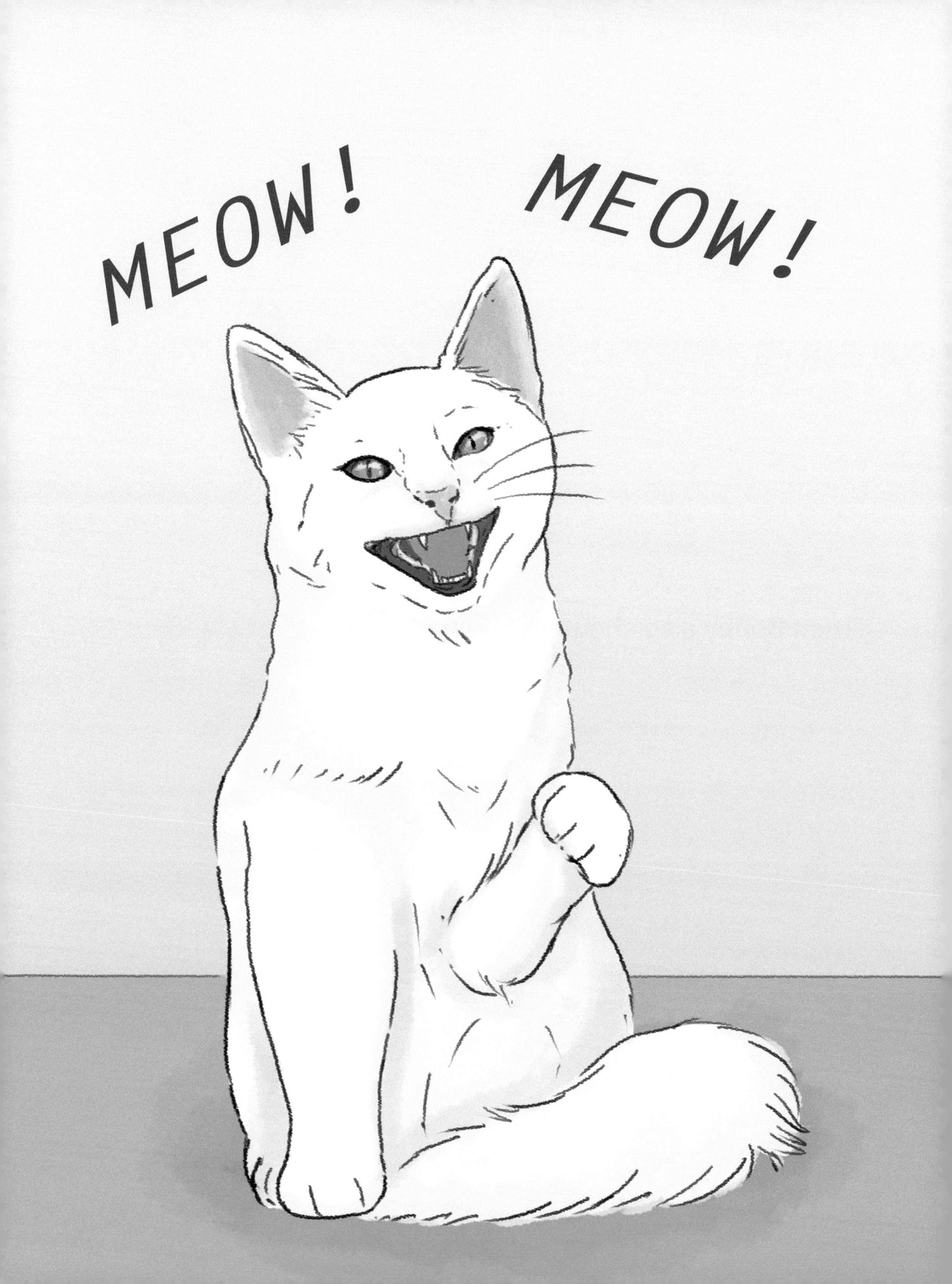
MEOW!
MEOW!

Then Bobby also shouted, "Happy birthday."

HAPPY BIRTHDAY!

Printed in the United States
by Baker & Taylor Publisher Services